CHARLIE
the Ranch Dog

For my children. And for Charlie.
—Mama

Charlie the Ranch Dog

Text copyright © 2011 by Ree Drummond
Illustrations copyright © 2011 by Diane deGroat
All rights reserved. Manufactured in China.
No part of this book may be used or reproduced in any manner whatsoever without
written permission except in the case of brief quotations embodied in critical articles
and reviews. For information address HarperCollins Children's Books, a division of
HarperCollins Publishers, 195 Broadway, New York, NY 10007.
www.harpercollinschildrens.com

Library of Congress Cataloging-in-Publication Data
Drummond, Ree.
Charlie the ranch dog / by Ree Drummond ; illustrations by Diane deGroat. —1st ed.
p.   cm.
Summary: The adventures of Charlie, basset hound ranch dog, and his sidekick, Suzie.
ISBN 978-0-06-199655-9 (trade bdg.)
[1. Ranch life—Fiction. 2. Basset hound—Fiction. 3. Jack Russell terrier—Fiction.
4. Dogs—Fiction.] I. De Groat, Diane, ill. II. Title.
PZ7.D8277Ch 2011   2010018435   [E]—dc22   CIP   AC

Typography by Rachel Zegar
19 20 SCP 20 19 18 17 16 15 14
❖
First Edition

When cooking, it is important to keep safety in mind. Children should always ask permission from an adult before
cooking and should be supervised by an adult in the kitchen at all times. The publisher and author disclaim any liability
from any injury that might result from the use, proper or improper, of the recipe contained in this book.

CHARLIE
the Ranch Dog

by Ree Drummond

illustrations by Diane deGroat

HARPER

An Imprint of HarperCollinsPublishers

Oh, hello.

My name is Charlie. I live in the country.
I'm a ranch dog.

This is Suzie.

She's my best friend.
We sure don't look much alike, do we?

Suzie, unfortunately, doesn't have the **paws** I have.

Or the droopy eyes.

Or the floppy skin.

Or . . . the big, dangly ears.

Suzie's ears don't dangle. Never have. Never will.

I try not to hold that against her.

But then again . . . Suzie sure can run.

And dig.

And jump.

BOING!

I've never been much of a jumper. Believe me, I've tried.
And tried . . . and tried . . . and tried.
The old legs just don't work that way.
But all that stuff doesn't really matter anyway. 'Cause
tall or short, slow or fast, tiny ears or floppy ears, there's
plenty of work around here for both of us.

The first thing we do every day is get out of bed early.

Too early.

Dark early.

I'd better go wake up Suzie. She's never been much of a morning dog.

Well . . . I guess she was a morning dog today.

There's a first time for everything, I suppose.

The next thing I have to do is chase Daisy the cow out of the yard.

Daisy *knows* she's not supposed to be in the yard.
Some cows never listen.

Well . . . I guess I'll let Suzie go ahead and do it this time.

I like to give her a chance to shine every now and then.
It's the kind of dog I am.

Alrighty, now that Daisy's under control, it's time for me to sniff the porch steps. I've got to keep all the critters out.

Sniffing the porch steps is hard work. Up and down and up and down,

sniff . . .

sniff . . .

sniff.

Sniff.

Sniff-sniff.

Sniff.

Yep. All clear down there.

It's a good thing I'm here to keep the critters away.

After the porch steps are good and sniffed, I like to stop and have my breakfast. I can't be expected to do all this work on an empty stomach.

Yum. Breakfast is my life.

After breakfast, I usually go help Mama in her vegetable garden. Mama *loves* her garden.

I don't really understand all the fuss. I'd prefer a *bacon* garden myself. But I go ahead and lend a hand anyway.

It sure is a good thing Mama has me to help her.
There's no way she'd get it all done without me.

It isn't even lunchtime yet, and I've already worked harder than most dogs out there.

I think I'll just sit down and rest for a minute.

I think I'll just . . .

just . . .

ZZZZZZZZZZZ . . .

Huh? What'd I miss?

Oh. I must have accidentally closed my eyes for a few seconds. I'd better get back to work!

Work, after all, is what I do best.

I have cattle to round up . . .

ZZZZZZzz . . .

fences to fix . . .

and fish to catch. I'm known for my expert fishing skills.

Eventually, we make our way back to the house. Suzie's ready to eat lunch by then.

I usually go ahead and eat, too.
I wouldn't want Suzie to have to dine alone.

After lunch, Suzie likes to lie down and take her afternoon nap. I usually go ahead and lie down, too.
I wouldn't want Suzie to have to nap . . . by . . .

herself.

ZZZzzzz . . .

Huh? What'd I miss?

Oh. I must have accidentally closed my eyes
for a few seconds.

Uh . . . Hello? Where'd everybody go?

Rats. I guess they went back to work without me.
Nothin' else to do but take another nap, I guess.

Wait . . . **what's that?**

Methinks I hear the sound of approaching beasts.

Whew. That was a close call.

It sure is a good thing I decided to stay home.
There's no telling what would have happened if
I hadn't been here.

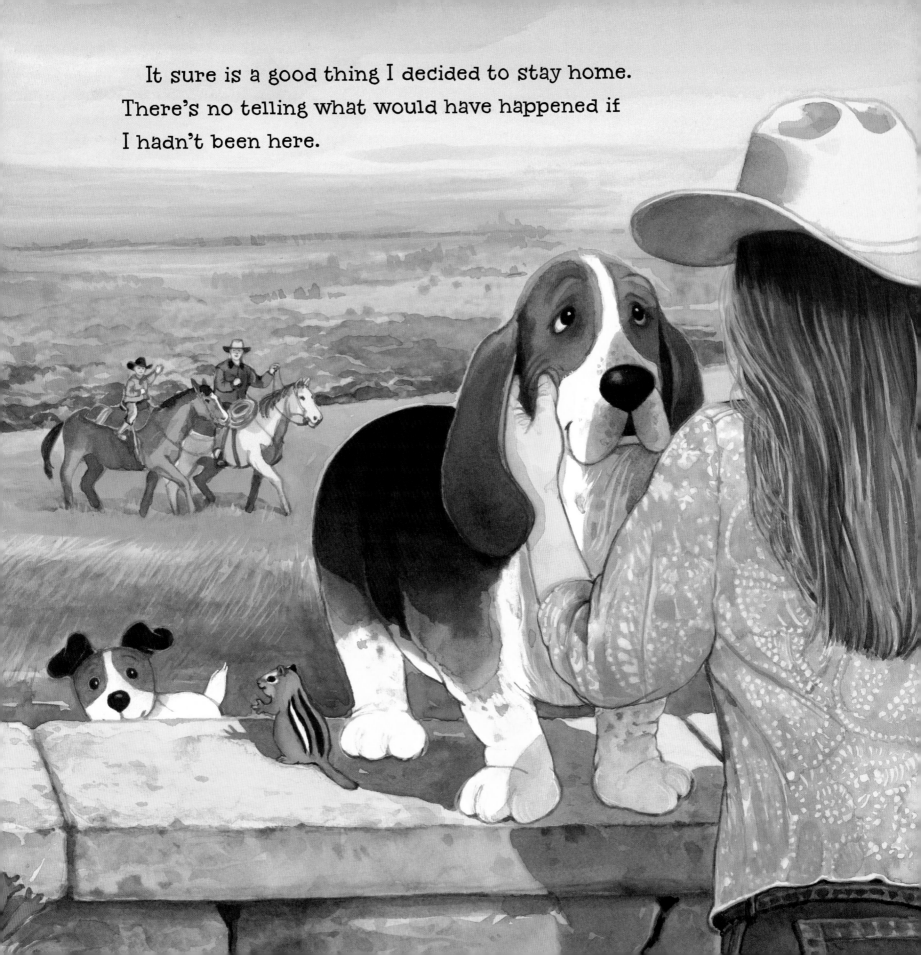

Now if you'll excuse me, I think I'll lie down and rest for a minute. I've had a long, hard day of work.

I just hope Suzie remembers to wake me up in time for dinner.

ZZZZZ

ZZZZZZ...

The Pioneer Woman's (and Charlie's) Favorite Lasagna

Makes 8 generous servings

Be safe! Always cook with an adult. Don't touch sharp knives or hot stoves and ovens! And always wash your hands before and after cooking.

Ingredients

1 (10-ounce) package lasagna noodles

1½ pounds ground beef

1 pound breakfast sausage

2 cloves garlic, minced

2 (14.5-ounce) cans whole tomatoes

2 (6-ounce) cans tomato paste

¼ cup minced parsley

10–12 basil leaves

1 teaspoon salt

3 cups low-fat cottage cheese

2 eggs, beaten

1 cup grated Parmesan cheese

2 additional tablespoons minced parsley

1 pound sliced mozzarella cheese

Extra Parmesan, for sprinkling

Instructions

1. Cook lasagna noodles according to package directions. Drain and lay flat on aluminum foil or a cookie sheet. Smile and wink at your doggie.

2. In a large skillet or saucepan, combine ground beef, sausage, and garlic. Cook over medium-high heat until meat is browned. Drain off half the fat. Add tomatoes, tomato paste, ¼ cup parsley, basil, and ½ teaspoon salt. Simmer for 45 minutes. Take your doggie for a walk.

3. In a medium bowl, mix cottage cheese, eggs, 1 cup Parmesan, 2 tablespoons minced parsley, and ½ teaspoon salt. Stir together well. Set aside.

4. To assemble, arrange 4 cooked lasagna noodles in the bottom of a deep rectangular baking pan, overlapping if necessary. Spoon half the cottage cheese mixture over the noodles. Spread evenly. Cover cottage cheese with a layer of mozzarella slices. Spoon a little less than half the meat/sauce mixture over the top. Repeat layers, ending with remaining meat/sauce mixture. Sprinkle top generously with extra Parmesan.

5. Either freeze, refrigerate for up to two days, or bake immediately in a 350-degree oven for 30 minutes, or until top is hot and bubbly. Tell your doggie it won't be long!

6. Allow to sit for 10 minutes before cutting into squares. Serve to hardworking humans . . . and doggies.